This book belongs to:

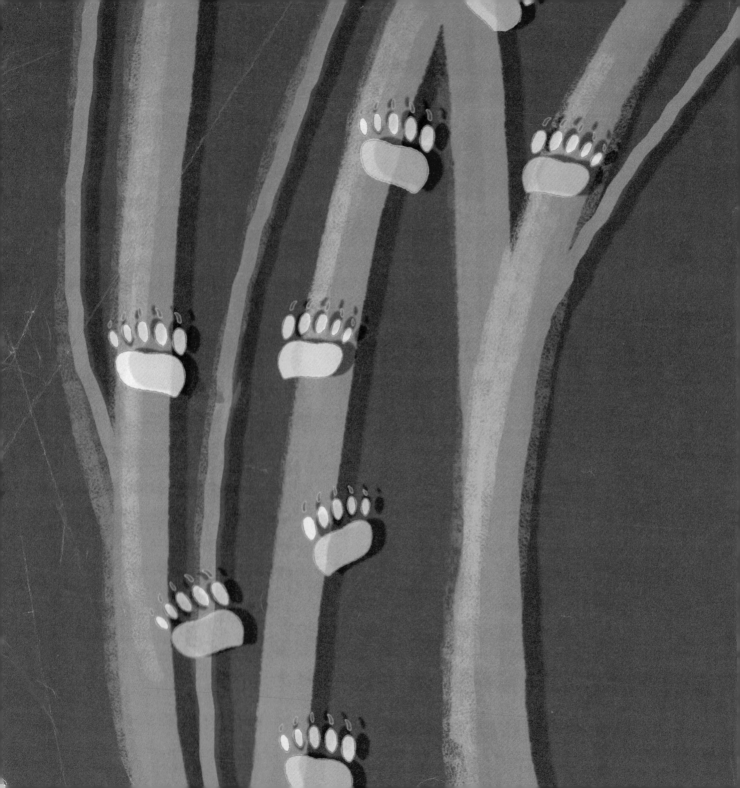

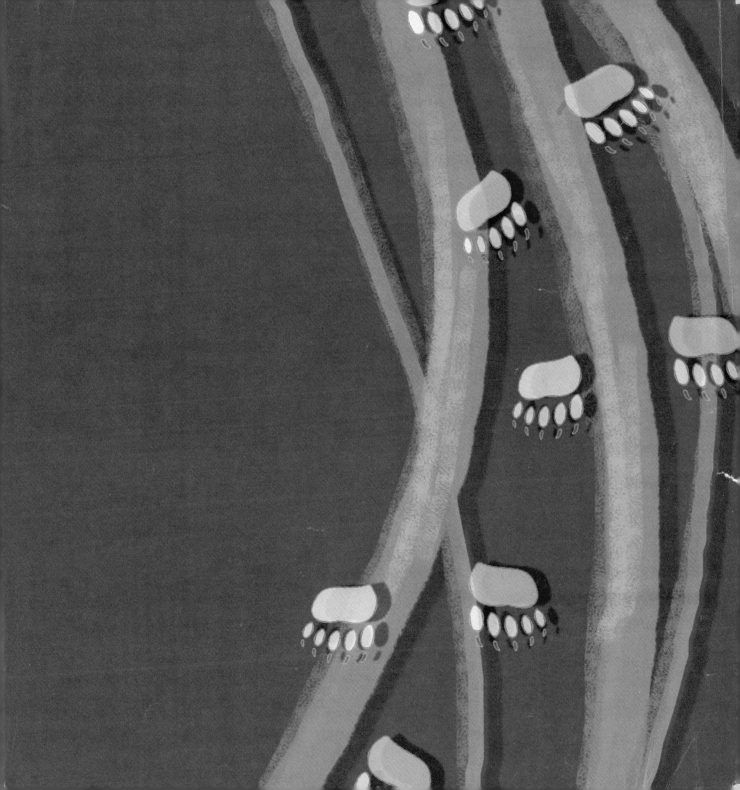

Cover design by Viktoriia Mykhalevych
Book design by Viktoriia Mykhalevych
Poetry by Trevor Judson and Agnes Green

Agnes Green
Visit my website at www.AprilTaleBooks.com

Printed in the United States of America
First Printing: November 2017
www.apriltalebooks.com

TODAY I'm A MONSTER

Trevor Judson
Agnes Green

Today I am a monster.
I woke with a sore head.
I want to keep on dreaming.
Don't get me out of bed!

I will not put my slippers on,
My claws won't fit inside,
Today I have my monster face,
You'd better run and hide!

I will not say good morning
to you, dear mom and dad.
I'd rather do a monster dance
to show you that I'm bad!

I will not eat my cereal...
And look, my bowl's a hat!
I'd rather eat it monster style,
then tip it on the cat.

My juice is the brightest orange...
The color of monster blood.
I'll pour some on the table cloth,
I'm sure you'll think it's good.

My sister built a Lego house
that took her all last week.
My monster foot stomps down on it,
and really makes her shriek!

We walk to kindergarten.
My neighbor says, "Hey you!"
Because I'm standing on his flowers
as angry monsters do.

"I like your lovely daffodils,
I love your climbing rose,
I think I'll pull the petals off,
and stick them up your nose!"

All the time the angry feeling's
hot within my head.
It wants to make me do bad things
that get me sent to bed.

Mother takes me to the park,
Our dog begins to wail.
"Hey! Don't you bite that poor pup,
and let go of his tail!"

We meet my friend and I grab his car.
He cries and pulls and pushes.
With monster strength, I tug it free,
and throw it in the bushes!

"I am the monster boy!" I shout,
all tired and forlorn.
"I'll eat you all and never sleep!"
Then I lay down on the lawn.

Mother sees I'm drifting off,
The monster's eyes can only peep.
She scoops me up and carries me,
And oh! Her hair smells just like sleep.

She carries me and puts me down,
Wraps me in my quilt.
She seems to know it was not me
who roared, and broke, and spilt.

She tells me that she knows I'm not
the thing with claws and teeth,
That when I'm angry,
she still sees the good boy underneath.

And as she softly cradles me,
I'm turning back into me.
Her love can melt through monsters.
The good is all she sees.

"Everyone has bad days,
All grown-ups know it's true
When I was just a little girl
I was a monster too!"

"But mothers know that monsters
are an angry old disguise.
The best of you is still inside.
We see it in your eyes."

"We love you when you make us proud,
We love you when you rage,
We soothe the monster with our love
and return it to its cage"

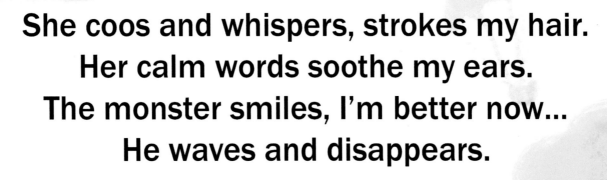

She coos and whispers, strokes my hair.
Her calm words soothe my ears.
The monster smiles, I'm better now...
He waves and disappears.

Sleep is coming, warm and quiet.
The slipping sunlight gleams,
I'm bobbing on a little boat
upon the sea of dreams.

I'll be me again tomorrow,
I'll play outside for hours,
I'll help my sister build her house,
And the neighbor with his flowers.

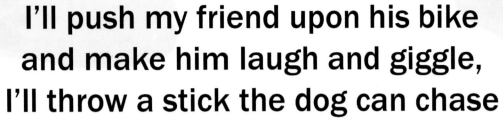

I'll push my friend upon his bike
and make him laugh and giggle,
I'll throw a stick the dog can chase
and give his chin a tickle.

And if my monster should come back
one angry, rainy day,
I'll give him half my lunch
and tell him, everything's okay.

THE

END

TODAY
I'M A MONSTER

"Coloring Pages & Activity Book"
is also avaliable for downloading
from my site:
www.apriltalebooks.com/coloring-pages

COLORING

PAGES

&

ACTIVITY

BOOK

Color ✏️ and Cut ✂️

Create your monster !

Thank you for reading!
I hope you enjoyed
this cute little story!

Reviews from awesome customers
like you help others to feel confident
about choosing this book too.

Please take a minute to review it
and share your experience!

Thank you in advance
for helping me out!
I will be forever grateful.

Yours,
Agnes Green
www.apriltalebooks.com

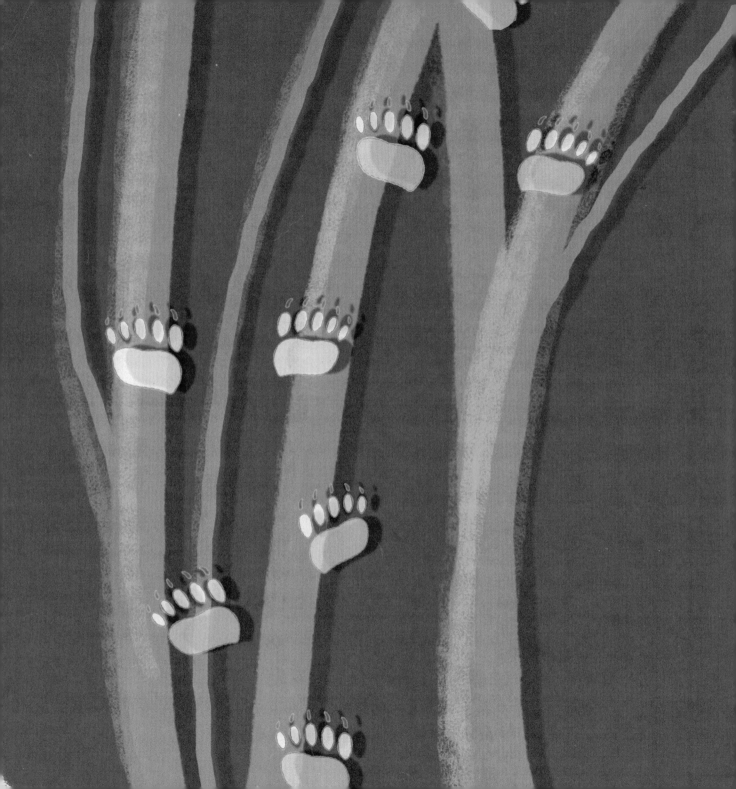

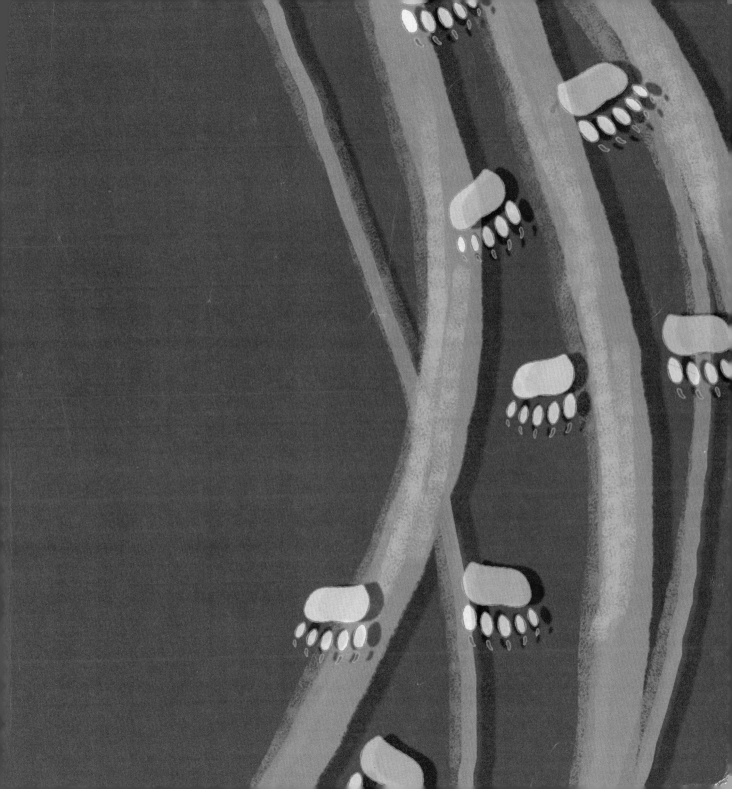

85659302R00024

Made in the USA
San Bernardino, CA
21 August 2018